my LITTLE PONY

CRYSTAL HEART
Kisses

Adapted by **Tallulah May**

Based on the episode "The Crystalling, Part One"

and "The Crystalling, Part Two"

by **Josh Haber**

LITTLE, BROWN & COMPANY

LB kids

Title font set in Generation B by Harold's Fonts

Little, Brown and Company

Hachette Book Group
1290 Avenue of the Americas, New York, NY 10104
Visit us at lb-kids.com
mylittlepony.com

LB kids is an imprint of Little, Brown and Company.
The LB kids name and logo are trademarks of Hachette Book Group, Inc.

The publisher is not responsible for websites (or their content) that are not owned by the publisher.

First Edition: December 2016

Library of Congress Control Number: 2016944308

ISBN 978-0-316-39527-4

10 9 8 7 6 5 4 3 2 1

CW

Printed in the United States of America

There's big news in Equestria! Princess Cadance and Shining Armor have a new baby, and everypony is invited to the Crystal Empire to celebrate with a big ceremony.

When the invitation arrives on a magical snowflake, Twilight Sparkle gets very excited!

"Um…what's a Crystalling?" Starlight Glimmer asks.

"We're not sure," Rarity says. "But we think it's got something to do with—"

"A *party!*" Pinkie Pie finishes.

Spike explains that whenever a baby is born in the Crystal Empire, the parents present the baby in front of the Crystal Heart. Then everypony at the Crystalling shares the love and joy they feel, which increases the Crystal Heart's power.

The ponies are all thrilled to attend such an important event.

On the train to the Crystal Kingdom, everypony shows off the presents they've brought for the new baby. Applejack made a cradle. Rainbow Dash brought a Cloudsdale mobile. Rarity sewed a stylish baby blanket.

"I'm sure Shining Armor and Princess Cadance will appreciate all our gifts, but they'll be happier we are sharing our love and joy at the baby's Crystalling," Twilight says.

But once they arrive, Shining Armor doesn't recognize his sister, Twilight. He looks so tired!

"Maybe you need some help…" Twilight says.
"And a nap."
"I'm so glad you're here," Shining Armor says.

At the castle, Shining Armor warns the group that the baby might be a little different from what they're expecting. Everypony is confused until he opens the door and they see the new baby.

She is an Alicorn!

"Wow," Pinkie Pie says. "A Unicorn *and* a Pegasus! She could be a superstrong flier *and* have crazy baby magic."

"Equestria has never seen a baby Alicorn before," Princess Celestia says.

Twilight Sparkle isn't worried. "We can handle it!" she says.

But suddenly the baby lets out a *huge* sneeze...and blows a hole straight through the ceiling!

"Maybe we'll need a little more help than I thought," Twilight says.

Rainbow Dash, Applejack, and Fluttershy go with Shining Armor to help him pick a crystal for the ceremony. Rarity brings Shining Armor a tray of beautiful sparklers for him to choose from.

"I've even arranged them for you from incredibly pure to outrageously pure," Rarity says.

But they all look the same to Shining Armor.

"*I can't decide!*" he cries out.

Once Shining Armor has calmed down, Pinkie Pie and Twilight show up with the baby. Or, really, the baby arrives carrying Pinkie Pie!

"She's a *really* strong flier!" says Pinkie Pie.

"I think that's enough fun for now," Princess Cadance says as she and the rest of the ponies join the group.

But as soon as the baby is separated from Pinkie Pie, she starts making a weird face. Then she starts crying. And then...she lets out a *supersonic baby wail!*

And the Crystal Heart cracks into a million tiny pieces!

"Oh no!" yells Twilight. "Without the Crystal Heart, the Empire will be buried under a mountain of ice and snow!"

"We might be able to find a spell to repair the Crystal Heart in the castle library," Princess Cadance says with a worried look on her face.

Twilight Sparkle vows to find the spell, and everypony wants to help.

But before they can start looking, the baby catches sight of Pinkie Pie and disappears from Shining Armor's hooves, only to reappear on Pinkie's head! Pinkie yelps in surprise, dropping the baby. But before she hits the ground, she disappears again!

The ponies hear giggling coming from the library and rush over to find the baby flying around the room, blasting magical holes through the castle walls. From outside, it looks like fireworks!

The baby is making it hard for Twilight to concentrate. But with Cadance's help, she manages to find the Spell of Relic Reconstitution.

"We found it just in time!" Twilight says. "Without this spell, I don't know what we'd do!"

But when Pinkie Pie catches the baby,
the tiny Alicorn sneezes and shoots out another
blast of magic, which...
    reflects off Rarity's mirror, which...
        flies off Shining Armor's shield, which...
            bounces off Starlight's magic dome...
                straight at the book!

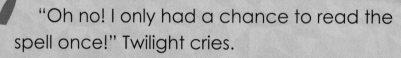

"Oh no! I only had a chance to read the spell once!" Twilight cries.

"I'll help if I can…" says Cadance uncertainly.

"Don't worry," says Shining Armor, giving Cadance a nuzzle. "Between you and Twilight, I'm sure you'll remember the spell."

"Maybe I can help," says Starlight. "My friend Sunburst knows every spell there is."

Starlight's friend Sunburst arrives just as Twilight and Cadance have finished writing down the spell.

"The Spell of Relic Reconstitution? This won't be strong enough to fix the Crystal Heart. If we combine this spell with the power of love, we can strengthen the Heart—"

"The Crystalling!" Twilight cries.

Sunburst carries the baby out in front of the crowd. Twilight Sparkle, Luna, Celestia and Starlight use the Spell of Relic Reconstitution to hold the Crystal Heart together. Cadance and Shining Armor both give the baby a big kiss, and their magic makes the baby float up over the crowd

Everypony in the crowd bows down to the new baby princess, sharing their love and joy, and creating a magical burst of energy that spreads out over the whole kingdom! The Crystal Heart is fixed!

The next day, Twilight and Shining Armor's parents finally arrive on the train.

"You wouldn't believe the weather we had!" Night Light says.

"But it was all worth it to see this little dear," coos Twilight Velvet. "What's her name?"

"Flurry Heart...to remember the occasion," says Cadance with a smile.

Twilight Sparkle thinks it's the perfect name.